DRAGONBREATH
KNIGHT-NAPPED!

DRAGONBREATH

KNIGHT-NAPPED!

BY

URSULA VERNON

DIAL BOOKS

an imprint of Penguin Group (USA) LLC

For Ben

DIAL BOOKS
Published by the Penguin Group • Penguin Group (USA) LLC
375 Hudson Street • New York, New York 10014

USA/Canada/UK/Ireland/Australia/New Zealand/India/South Africa/China
PENGUIN.COM
A Penguin Random House Company

Library of Congress Cataloging-in-Publication Data
Vernon, Ursula.
 Knight-napped! / by Ursula Vernon.
  pages cm. — (Dragonbreath ; 10)
Summary: "Danny Dragonbreath must save his cousin from the ultimate enemy: knights!"
—Provided by publisher.
 ISBN 978-0-8037-3849-2
[1. Dragons—Fiction. 2. Knights and knighthood—Fiction. 3. Cousins—Fiction.
4. Adventure and adventurers—Fiction.] I. Title.
PZ7.V5985Kni 2015
 [Fic]—dc23
 2013027094

Printed in the United States of America

10 9 8 7 6 5 4 3 2 1

Designed by Jennifer Kelly
Text set in Stempel Schneidler

HE WAS SO COOL THAT—

—SO COOL THAT—

—THAT—

A NEW DANCE

The bird was large and gray and had a purplish-greenish shine across its feathers. It was definitely a pigeon.

It was also very definitely sitting on Danny's head.

"Technically it's a rock dove," said Wendell the iguana helpfully. "*Columba livia,* to be exact. They nest on cliffs, and when people started building skyscrapers, the pigeons starting nesting on those too."

"Wendell," said Danny.

"Yes?"

"*Why* is there a pigeon on my head?"

Wendell rubbed his chin. "Good question. Maybe it thought your head looked like the Empire State Building?"

NOT HELPING, WENDELL!

Danny Dragonbreath had enough problems. He was the only dragon in a school full of frogs and lizards, he couldn't breathe fire very well, and he was pretty sure that he had just flunked a pop quiz. Having a pigeon on his head was one problem too many.

He tried to pull it off. It latched on to his scales with its feet and made happy pigeon noises.

"I think it likes you," said Wendell.

"Get it off!" yelled Danny. "Lunch will be over any minute now! I can't go back to class with a pigeon on my head!"

"Errr . . . tell everyone it's a hat?" Wendell flapped his hands at the pigeon. "Go on, shoo!"

The two-minute bell rang in the distance.

The pigeon finally got the hint and took off, flapping. "Coo!" it said reproachfully.

"That was weird," said Wendell. "Even by your standards."

Danny rubbed his head and grumbled.

They were nearly back to class when a familiar shape loomed in front of them.

"Hey, Dorkbreath," said Big Eddy.

"Big Eddy," said Danny.

WHAT WAS THAT ALL ABOUT? YOU DOIN' SOME KIND OF DANCE?

He poked Danny in the chest with one finger. Since Big Eddy was a Komodo dragon, his fingers were the size of bratwurst. "You a *dancer* now, Dorkbreath? You gonna invent a new dance and put a video on the Internet so we can all laugh at you?"

He poked Danny again.

"We're gonna be late . . ." mumbled Wendell, trying to slide sideways around Big Eddy.

Danny rolled his eyes. "*Obviously* there was a pigeon on my head. You need to pay closer attention."

Big Eddy blinked.

The school bully was very large but not very bright. It was sometimes possible to stun him by uttering something so unexpected that he took a few minutes to process it.

"Pigeon?" he said.

"It's a new thing. Head-pigeoning. I thought you would have heard of it by now."

"Head-pigeoning?"

The bell rang again.

"Gotta go!" said Danny, and ran off to find out how badly he'd flunked the quiz.

A STRANGE MESSAGE

Danny and Wendell got off at the bus stop near Danny's house. The dragon got about five steps before something warm and feathery settled on his head.

"It's the pigeon again, isn't it?" said Danny grimly.

"Yep," said Wendell. "Or *a* pigeon, anyway. I suppose there could be more than one."

This was not reassuring.

Danny hunched his shoulders and stalked down the sidewalk. There was probably no point in trying to get it off until he was close enough to the house to duck inside.

A passing car slowed down to stare at him.

Danny was no stranger to having cars slow down to stare at him, but usually it was because he was doing something awesome like standing on a rooftop wearing a cape or building a giant snow platypus. Merely having a pigeon on his head didn't qualify.

"Wendell! Hey, Wendell!"

Wendell slowed down. Danny sighed and turned around.

Christiana Vanderpool, the only person in school nerdier than Wendell, ran down the sidewalk after them. "Hey, Wendell, can I borrow that book on the Burgess Shale?"

"Sure!" said Wendell.

"The what?" said Danny.

"Very old rock. Had lots of squirmy things fossilized in it. Stuff nobody's ever seen on earth before. Or since, for that matter." She paused. "Did you know there's a pigeon on your head?"

NO, REALLY?

"*Columba livia*—"

"Yeah yeah, so Wendell said."

"Quite a nice specimen," said Christiana. She stood on her tiptoes and scratched the pigeon's head. "*Who's* a good widdle pigeon, den?"

"You want the pigeon? It's yours. You can teach it to fly mazes or something." Danny tried to pry the pigeon off his head again. It flapped hard a few times, then snuggled down against his scales.

"I think it likes you," said Christiana.

"Yeah, it sat on my head at recess too."

"Is *this* why Big Eddy was wandering around with bread crumbs on his head? I was wondering about that, but I didn't want to ask him."

"Did it work?" asked Wendell.

"Well . . . sort of. . . ." She scratched her head. "He didn't get pigeons, he got starlings. A bunch of them. And you know what they do when they get excited . . ."

"Squawk?" guessed Danny.

She gave him a look. "No. They poop."

"The pigeon followed Danny home from school," said Wendell proudly. "And it hasn't pooped on him *once.*"

"Maybe it's a homing pigeon," said Christiana. "Although they usually go to places, not to people. There are reports of homing pigeons flying thousands of miles with important messages. They navigate by magnetic fields."

"Hey, that's a good thought," said Wendell. "We should check it for messages."

"Why would someone send a homing pigeon after me?" asked Danny. "I don't know any pigeons." He paused. "Unless . . . there's an evil genius about to take over the world using pigeons, and this one's just the first, and pretty soon *everybody* will have a pigeon on their head and then we'll be helpless when he deploys his orbital moon laser!"

"Or *her* orbital moon laser," said Christiana. "I hear more women are breaking into mad science all the time."

WOULDN'T IT MAKE MORE SENSE TO USE SOMETHING PEOPLE ARE ACTUALLY SCARED OF, LIKE WOLVERINES?

WE'D BE HAVING A TOTALLY DIFFERENT CONVERSATION IF YOU HAD A WOLVERINE ON YOUR HEAD.

LOOK, WHEN WE'RE ALL COVERED IN HEAD-PIGEONS, DON'T SAY I DIDN'T WARN YOU.

"There's a note tied to its leg," said Christiana. "C'mon, little guy, let me just untie this . . . *there's* a good pigeon . . ."

The note was tiny and rolled up like a scroll. She smoothed it out and handed it to Danny. "It's addressed to you."

Danny scratched his head, moving the pigeon slightly. "Okay . . ."

Dear Danny,

Help! I am stuck in a castle full of knights and they say they're going to slay me. I don't know the name of the castle, but all the flags have a spotted chicken and a carrot on them. I am in a tower and it is drafty and cold and there is no TV.

Whatever you do, DON'T TELL MOM!

Love,

Spencer

P.S. The pigeon's name is Fluffy.

"Fluffy?" said Danny. "Who names a pigeon *Fluffy?*"

Fluffy the pigeon cooed happily at him.

"Seriously, you'd name a pigeon—Flappy or Pidgy or—or—Mister Feathers, not—"

"Not to interrupt," said Wendell, "but your cousin Spencer has apparently been kidnapped."

"Oh, yeah, that." Danny shrugged. If there had been a world championship for Most Annoying Cousin, Spencer would win every time. Then he'd whine until somebody carried the trophy for him. "I mean, I suppose that's awful . . . in theory . . ."

"I thought you were friends after we all went to Camp Jackalope together," said Wendell.

"Yeah. Then he came over for three days at Thanksgiving and made that *wa-waaaaah* . . . noise every time I died playing *Super Mech Unleashed*. And then when I tried to get him to stop, he told his mom, and his mom told *my* mom, and there was a lecture about sharing and—look, we sort of un-bonded."

"A spotted chicken and a carrot . . ." said Christiana to no one in particular.

"You can't let your cousin get slain by knights."

"They probably won't slay him. Anyway, knights are an endangered species. If they need to kidnap Spencer to survive, it's the circle of life or something. I can't believe, after all the times you've been like *'Nooo, Danny, we can't interfere with the natural order!'* that you want me to go pester some knights."

"You wanted to cross my goldfish with a potato!"

"I was going to start a mutant fish-and-chip farm."

"You were using *masking tape.*"

"I suppose it wouldn't hurt to go check it out," Danny said. "But how do we find the castle?"

"Heraldry," said Wendell. "We'll go to the library and find a book on heraldry, and we'll see who has a spotted chicken and a carrot on their coat of arms, then we'll look up their castle—"

"It's Castle Wanderpoll," said Christiana. "And it's not a carrot, it's a parsnip."

WHAT?

"How did you *know* that?" asked Danny.

"Did you have to do a paper on coats of arms?" asked Wendell.

"Um," said Christiana. "Not exactly . . . ?"

A SURPRISE ANCIENT ENEMY

"So let me get this straight . . ." said Danny.

Christiana sighed.

"Your family just happens to own a *castle?*"

"Not *my* family," said Christiana. "I mean, *we* don't own the castle. We don't even own our house. But—look, you remember in fourth grade when we had to do the project where you draw your family tree and write everybody's names down?"

"I remember," said Wendell.

Danny had a hard time remembering homework from the day before, let alone from previous grades. He moved the pigeon to the other side of his head. His scales were getting sweaty.

"Right," said Christiana. "So I went digging and apparently 'Vanderpool' used to be pronounced *Wanderpoll* and there was a coat of arms with a chicken and a parsnip and a knighthood and a castle. I've never been there. We're only sort of related. They're like my great-great-great-cousins eight or nine times removed. But . . . well . . ."

NO WONDER WE'VE ALWAYS HAD A HARD TIME GETTING ALONG . . .

EH?

KNIGHTS . . .
DRAGONS . . .
YOU KNOW!

"I guess it can't hurt to go to the castle and look around," said Danny. He sighed. He knew that if Spencer really was in trouble, he'd have to rescue him—it was just what you did—but the thought that Spencer might be locked in a tower over, say, the critical week of spring break when he usually visited Danny, was certainly appealing.

But his aunt would probably worry. And then she'd tell Danny's mom and Danny's mom would have a Talk with him about Why We Do Not Go Off and Leave Our Cousins in Horrible Danger. He sighed again.

"We'll go tell my mom," he said. "You guys can call from our house."

"Is your mom going to let you stay at a castle overnight?" asked Christiana as they walked in Danny's front door.

"Sure," said Danny. "This is the easy part."

HEY, MOM! CAN I GO SPEND THE NIGHT AT CHRISTIANA'S COUSIN'S PLACE? IT'S A CASTLE!

"Sure," his mom called from her office. "A castle! Sounds exciting!"

Christiana stared at him. "I don't even know these cousins!"

"It'll be fine," said Danny. He shoved most of a box of snack cakes into his backpack. "We'll just take some food in case we miss dinner."

He zipped up the backpack just as his mom entered the room.

She was carrying a coffee mug. She looked at Danny and tilted her head slowly to one side.

SON, I REALIZE I'M GOING TO REGRET ASKING THIS, BUT... WHY IS THERE A PIGEON ON YOUR HEAD?

"It's School Spirit Week," said Danny. "You know. Tuesday was 'wear pajamas to school' day, and Friday was 'wear a pigeon on your head' day."

Mrs. Dragonbreath's gaze traveled slowly over to Christiana.

"Don't look at me," said the crested lizard. "I don't do Spirit Week. It's like brainwashing without the fun bits."

Danny's mother went to the coffeemaker. "In my day we just dressed up like our favorite fictional character," she said. "Getting old, I guess . . . Have fun storming the castle . . ."

"Thanks, Mom!"

It took three bus transfers to get to Castle Wanderpoll.

"Not bad for a castle that's technically in Austria," said Wendell.

"It's a good bus system," said Danny.

They both looked at Christiana and waited for her to protest how impossible it all was.

She stared out the window and didn't say anything.

This was worrisome.

She didn't say anything when they got on the bus. She didn't say anything when they got off the bus. She didn't say anything when they got on the next bus, or the one after that.

The bus drivers *did* say something, but that was another matter.

(That last bit was particularly annoying. Danny had to pretend to be blind for the entire bus trip, and Wendell had to lead him to his seat.)

"You think Christiana's okay?" whispered Wendell.

"How should I know?" Danny whispered back. "She's not yelling at me, so that's probably a bad sign."

"Sorry," said Wendell. "But you haven't said anything for hours. I mean, we transferred at the Black Forest and the Carpathian Mountains, and you didn't say a word."

"Oh. Right." She waved a hand. "It's impossible. Laws of physics. Buses. Very upsetting. Completely unprecedented. Et cetera."

She went back to staring out the window.

Danny and Wendell exchanged concerned looks. This wasn't like Christiana at all. Normally if you broke the laws of physics around her, you needed a signed note from the universe saying that it was okay.

"Is something bothering you?" asked Wendell worriedly.

Christiana finally stopped looking out the window and turned around to glare at them.

"No, I'm just fine! Finding out that your relatives are in the habit of kidnapping little kids and imprisoning them in towers isn't upsetting in the least!"

"Look," said Danny awkwardly, "it's not like it's . . . y'know . . . a *normal* little kid. It's Spencer. I'm not saying it's not *bad,* but . . . well . . ."

"It's *Spencer,*" said Wendell.

"This is not a compelling ethical argument," said Christiana, but she looked a little more cheerful anyway.

"Besides," said Danny, "for all we know, we'll get there and they won't really have kidnapped him. He'll be sitting in the basement watching cartoons."

"You're right," said Christiana, sitting up straighter. "This could all just be a misunderstanding. A good scientist shouldn't make assumptions until she has all the facts." She nodded once. "Thanks, Danny."

Being thanked by Christiana was such a novel sensation that Danny was too busy enjoying it to say anything else until the bus driver called "Castle Wanderpoll!"

They had arrived.

FLUFFY TO THE RESCUE

Castle Wanderpoll was *perfect*.

If you were going to take a photo of a castle to go in the dictionary next to the word "castle" you couldn't do any better than Wanderpoll. Danny, Wendell, and Christiana stood at the foot of the road leading to the castle and stared up at it.

"Wow," said Danny.

"That's the place," said Christiana. "Parsnip flag and everything."

"Looks more like an example of Cathar architecture than Austrian," said Wendell.

"I wonder if it's got a moat!" said Danny.

"Moats are a pain in the tail," said Wendell. "I wouldn't have a moat. They'd always be flooding the basement or getting algae or something."

"But castles have to have moats! Otherwise they're just . . . big . . . stone . . . thingies! Where would you put the moat monster?"

"Can't I have a sidewalk monster instead?"

Christiana chewed on her lower lip. "Well, this is the castle . . . but how do we tell if Spencer's inside?"

"We could go up and ask . . ." said Wendell dubiously.

Danny shook his head. Wendell was brilliant, but he was also a little too likely to trust grown-ups. "If they really have kidnapped Spencer—and I'm not saying they didn't have a good reason—but just in case, it probably isn't smart to go up and say 'Hey, are you holding my cousin prisoner?' We might end up kidnapped too."

MAYBE EVEN IN THE SAME CELL AS SPENCER.

All three shuddered.

"And if they didn't do it, they might be very upset," said Christiana. "Accusing people of kidnapping is serious."

"Do we go up and look in the windows?" asked Wendell. "Only Spencer's note said he was in the tower, and that's a long way up . . ."

Danny scratched underneath Fluffy. The pigeon cooed.

"Maybe we could call the castle and ask to speak to Spencer . . ." Christiana said.

"That's it!" said Danny.

"What, call the castle?"

"Not that! *Fluffy!*" said Danny. He looked up toward the bird. "Hey, Fluffy . . . Good pigeon. *Nice* pigeon. You're a homing pigeon, aren't you?"

"Coo?"

"So you can home in on Spencer, right?"

"It doesn't work like that," said Wendell. "They find places, not people."

"Fluffy found me, didn't he?" said Danny. "He's clearly a genius pigeon. Aren't you, Fluffy?"

"Coo!"

"I think that's an oxymoron," said Christiana.

"*You're* an oxymoron. Don't listen to them, Fluffy." Danny prodded the pigeon. "Now go! Go find Spencer! Be a good pigeon!"

Fluffy shifted from foot to foot, cooing uncertainly.

"You think that'll work?" asked Christiana. "I mean, fine, okay, I've seen you talk to rats, but pigeons . . . ?"

"My dad always says pigeons are rats with wings," said Danny.

"My mom says pigeons are beautiful expressions of nature's infinite wonderment," said Wendell gloomily.

"Harsh," said Danny. Christiana winced.

Fluffy, however, seemed to enjoy being called an expression of nature's infinite wonderment. He stood up straighter and flapped a few times.

"Good pigeon! Nice pigeon! *Who's* a good pigeon that can go find cousin Spencer?"

Just when Danny was starting to think that he was standing in the woods, flattering a bird for no good reason, the pigeon spread its wings and launched itself off Danny's head.

Fluffy flapped furiously.

THAT'S RIGHT!
GO FIND SPENCER!

The trio watched as the pigeon gained altitude, sweeping in a broad circle around Castle Wander-poll.

Up it went, and around—once, twice—and then landed on a ledge at the window of the high-est tower.

They were too far away to see if anyone came to meet the bird, but after a minute or two it became obvious that it wasn't coming back.

"Well," said Danny. "I guess that proves it."

"It proves that the pigeon went back to Castle Wanderpoll," said Christiana. "It doesn't prove he went back to Spencer—although that does seem logical—and it still doesn't prove that Spencer's being held prisoner."

"Looks like there's only one way to find out for sure," said Danny.

STORMING THE CASTLE

"Lizard Scout Cookies?" asked Wendell. "Really?"

"Do you have a better plan?" asked Danny. "Besides, you know how it is—they take the orders first and then deliver them later. We'll just take the order. We don't actually need the cookies."

"How does that get us inside?" asked Wendell. "When you order Lizard Scout Cookies, the Scouts stay at the door."

"We're just doing reconnaissance," said Danny loftily.

Christiana looked at him suspiciously. "Do you even know what 'reconnaissance' means?"

"Sure," said Danny, who had seen it in a number of video games. "It's when you go sneaking around to see what's where. People do it before military missions and stuff."

"Aren't Lizard Scouts usually girls?" asked Wendell dubiously. "And don't they wear uniforms?"

"We'll tell them our uniforms are in the wash," said Danny.

"And don't you forget it," growled Christiana.

Danny was just glad she wasn't moping anymore. Christiana being quiet and miserable was *weird*.

They tromped up the road toward the castle. It was an old gravel road, with deep ruts and pebbles that glistened like a toad's warts in the sun.

"We'll take the order," said Danny. "And we'll ask how many people are in the castle, and if any of *them* would like to order cookies."

"Then what?" asked Wendell.

"Uh . . ." Danny scratched his head. It felt cold without the pigeon.

"We could build a giant box of cookies out of wood, climb inside, and leave it outside the walls," said Christiana. "Then when they bring it inside, we sneak out."

Wendell snickered. "Trojan cookies!"

Danny shook his head slowly. "Seriously, all that nerd brain power and *that's* the best you can come up with?"

"It has great historical precedent," said Wendell with dignity.

"Maybe Christiana could go in and say 'Hi, I'm your long-lost cousin . . .'" Danny offered.

Christiana shook her head. "No! What if they turn out to be kidnappers after all? What if they've got a weird family cult or start demanding DNA samples or put me on a Christmas newsletter mailing list or something?"

"Don't look now," said Wendell, pointing, "but that's a bad sign."

Wendell frowned and rubbed his snout with one hand. "But that doesn't make any sense!" he said. "If there are no dragons allowed, why would Spencer be there? He's a dragon!"

"Maybe he's not here," said Christiana hopefully. "Maybe it was a stupid prank and he trained a pigeon for it and nobody's been kidnapped and now we can go home."

"Pfff!" Danny marched past the sign. "Where's your sense of adventure? We're at a real castle! Run by your relatives! Don't you want to meet them?"

"Not really," said Christiana, following him. "Who says my relatives are nice people? I mean, Spencer's *your* relative, and you're not exactly best buddies."

Danny was forced to yield to the logic of this observation.

Wendell stayed staring at the sign for a moment longer, then ran after the other two, still frowning and deep in thought.

"It seems so specific," he said. "I wonder if Spencer saw it?"

"Spencer is bad about noticing when he's not welcome."

As they walked toward the castle, they discovered it had a moat. Danny was ecstatic.

Sure, it was only half-full, and the water was green and slimy and had an old tire floating in it, and sure, the drawbridge had been down for so long that it had rusted in place and somebody had put traffic cones in front of it and a little sign that said THIS IS NOT A PARKING SPOT, but that didn't matter.

"It's still a moat!" said Danny, delighted.

"I suppose for some value of 'moat,' you're correct," said Christiana.

"I think I'm behind on my tetanus shots," said Wendell, peering in. "And hepatitis shots. And . . . err . . . moat-fever shots. . . ."

Mosquitoes buzzed over the surface of the slimy water. Bubbles trailed up from the depths and burst with a wet popping sound.

"What do you think is *in* it?" asked Danny.

They came to a huge door with big iron studs and wrought iron knockers. That would have been cool, except . . .

DUDE! THAT IS NOT COOL!

The door knocker was in the shape of a dragon, twisted around, with a sword rammed right through it.

"I dunno, it's kinda wicked-looking," said Wendell, "but I guess I wouldn't like it if it was an iguana with a sword through it."

"Are we going to knock?" asked Christiana.

Danny scowled. He didn't approve of people having impaled dragons on their doors. He balled up a fist and hammered on the wood instead.

BOOM!

BOOM!

BOOM!

"There's a sign that says No Soliciting," said Wendell worriedly, pointing to a small sign beside the door.

"Good thing we're just selling cookies," said Danny.

"Selling cookies *is* soliciting," said Christiana.

"Good thing they're fake cookies, then."

After a long moment, they heard a bolt being drawn back, and the door creaked open.

"Lizard Scout Cookies!" the trio chorused.

The door opened a little wider.

"We're not soliciting," said Danny. "We're selling Lizard Scout Cookies."

Christiana sighed.

The knight stared at Danny for a long moment. "Aren't you supposed to be in uniform?"

"They're in the wash," said Danny. He tucked his tail behind him to keep the dragonish point from being obvious.

"And aren't Lizard Scouts usually girls?"

"Uh—"

"We're an equal opportunity organization," said Wendell firmly.

"Today's Lizard Scouts refuse to be bound by stereotypical gender roles," said Christiana. "You want some cookies or not?"

The knight considered this. "Do you have the mint ones? With the little frosting squiggles?"

"Mint Squigglies," said Wendell. "Sure. Shall I put you down for a dozen boxes?"

"Yes, please," said the knight. His gaze crept back to Danny. "Do I know you? You look awfully familiar . . ."

"Did you buy cookies last year?" asked Danny, thinking quickly.

"No . . ."

"Twelve boxes of Mint Squigglies," said Wendell, pretending to make notes in his geometry notebook. "And is there anyone else in the castle who might like some cookies?"

"I could *swear* I know you from somewhere . . ." muttered the knight.

"Anything else?" asked Wendell, a bit desperately. "Chocolate Moon Puffs? Peanut Butter Crunchie-Wunchies?"

"Are you sure twelve boxes will be enough?" asked Danny. "If you've got a lot of people in the castle, they may all want some!"

OR ANY KIDS? ABOUT NINE YEARS OLD, SAY? FOND OF VIDEO GAMES AND CARTOONS? THEY CAN GO THROUGH A BOX OF MINT SQUIGGLIES LIKE YOU WOULDN'T BELIEVE!

The knight blinked. His gaze traveled over Danny, from the top of the dragon's head down to the tip of his tail . . . which Danny had forgotten to keep tucked out of sight.

Wendell opened his mouth. Danny knew that the iguana was about to say something brainy, something brilliant, something that would get them out of trouble.

Unfortunately the knight grabbed Danny by one arm and Wendell by the other and dragged them both inside the castle before the iguana could say more than "Wait—hey—*ouch!*"

DUNGEONS AND LACKEYS

Danny had always wanted to be in a dungeon.

Dungeons were cool. They had cells with bars and rattling chains and moldy straw and weird wooden contraptions that probably did something horrible if you could just figure out how the levers worked.

Being locked in a dungeon was even better. As stories go, "So there I was, *locked in the dungeon*" was way cooler than "So there I was, touring the dungeon on a school field trip . . ."

He had to admit, though, being locked in the

dungeon was way more exciting in theory than in practice. In theory there had been dark deeds and daring escapes. In practice, he and Wendell and Christiana sat around in the straw—which wasn't moldy, although it was rather itchy—and played a game. The game was called "What Time Is It Now?" and no one was enjoying it.

"No way," said Danny. "It feels like *days.*"

"You have no idea . . ." said Christiana, not quite under her breath.

Danny sighed. "It was nice of you to get locked up with us," he admitted. "I mean, you didn't *have* to kick that knight in the shins like that."

"Although if you'd run away before the other knights showed up to grab you, you could have gone for help," said Wendell.

"We're in Austria," said Christiana, "in the middle of nowhere. Assuming I could even find somebody, they'd probably speak German or Serbian, and my Serbian is a little rusty." She wiggled her toes in the straw. "Besides, even if I found the police, they'd call my dad, and I'd have to explain why I was a trans-Atlantic flight away, and it would all get very complicated."

Wendell opened his mouth and then shut it again. On the one hand, it was nice that Christiana had finally accepted that buses acted weird around Danny. On the other hand, he had been about to point out that they might not even be in the real Austria, but in a weird mythological historical Austria, and that would probably strain Christiana's credibility a little too much.

"One of these days, Danny, we're going to have

to figure out how you make buses do that," said Christiana, as if reading Wendell's mind.

"I don't do anything," said Danny. "It's a good bus system."

... UH–HUH.

"Anyway," said Christiana, "I think we're going to have to figure this one out for ourselves." She scowled at the bars.

"They're knights," said Danny. "I'm a dragon."
The other two looked at him blankly.

WE'RE
ANCIENT ENEMIES!
KNIGHTS SLAY DRAGONS!
DRAGONS ROAST KNIGHTS!
IT'S WHAT THEY DO!

"*You've* never roasted a knight," said Wendell.

"Up until today, I'd never even seen one," Danny admitted. "They're an endangered species or something. Granddad Turlingsward is always going on about knights, though. I think it's an old-people thing, like the Great Depression. And rotary phones."

He wouldn't have minded roasting the knight that had dragged him and Wendell into the castle, but he was never very good at breathing fire reliably. And then once they were inside, there had been more knights, all of them very tall and grown-up looking.

Danny knew that once you started setting fire to grown-ups, you got in trouble so deep they had special words for it, like "delinquent" and "juvenile hall." Being in a dungeon was *nothing* compared to what his mom would do if she found out he'd been randomly breathing fire on people.

"Think Spencer's in this dungeon too?" asked Wendell.

Danny looked up, startled.

"I don't see any windows for pigeons," said Christiana, "and I think we're below the level of the moat. But it couldn't hurt to check."

Danny jumped to his feet and leaned out between the bars.

SPENCER! HEY, SPENCER! CAN YOU HEAR ME!?

His voice echoed from the stone walls, but the echoes were the only response.

Danny tried again—"*Spencer!* Yell back if you can hear me! It's Danny!"

Nothing.

"I don't think he's down here," said Wendell.

"Looks like you got somebody else's attention, though," said Christiana as the door to the hall creaked open.

A knight clanked through the doorway and up to the bars. It was hard to tell if it was the same one who had met them at the door. They all looked alike in their armor.

He was followed by another, identical knight. They closed the door and peered into the cell.

WHY ARE YOU HERE?

"Because you grabbed us and put us in a cell," said Danny. *"Obviously."*

The knights exchanged looks.

"The heads of twenty-seven dragons are mounted in the castle library," said one of them, in conversational tones, "and we would be happy to add a twenty-eighth to the collection. I suggest you answer a bit more respectfully."

"Twenty-seven—" Danny's jaw dropped. "You've—*twenty-seven*—!? *Those are my relatives, you jerk!*"

"Calm down!" hissed Christiana. "You're not gonna help anybody if you're stuffed and mounted in the library!"

"We're here looking for someone," said Wendell hurriedly. "A little kid named Spencer."

The knights exchanged looks again.

Danny shook off Christiana and lunged for the bars.

One of the knights took a step back.

"He's a feisty one," said the other knight.

"Relax, dragon, we haven't done anything to Spencer. Yet. He's being treated very well."

"Then why don't you let him go home?" demanded Danny.

It was hard to tell with the helmet, but Danny thought the knight smiled.

Danny grabbed both the bars in his hands. That didn't sound good at all.

"Fine!" he said, smoke pouring out of his nostrils. "I'm a dragon! Let Spencer go!"

The knights looked at him thoughtfully for a moment.

"You're a bit large," said one finally.

"We need a *small* dragon. The smaller the better, frankly."

That didn't sound good.

Before Danny could say anything else, though, Christiana shoved him aside.

YOU!
DO YOU KNOW WHO I AM?

If this lack of recognition bothered Christiana, she didn't give a sign. She drew herself up to her full height (four feet, ten and three-quarter inches) and said "I am Christiana Vanderpool, descended from the House of Wanderpoll. Release us *immediately!*"

The knights took a step back.

They looked at each other.

They scurried out through the door, clanking and rattling like a box full of frying pans.

Christiana sagged. "Darn. I really thought that might work."

"It was looking good," said Wendell. "But hey, at least we know Spencer's *here*. And they haven't done anything to him."

Danny swallowed his smoke and slumped into the straw. "Yeah, but they said they wanted a small dragon? I don't like the sound of that at *all*."

"Maybe . . . err . . . maybe they just want to have a really small weenie roast?" asked Wendell hopefully.

"Maybe they've got a really small corner of the library and only an extra-small dragon head will fit."

The door swung open again. With a clatter of armor, no fewer than *four* knights entered the hall.

A knight with an elaborately plumed helmet was in the lead. His armor looked old, and what little they could see of his face was lined.

He was holding a rubber chicken and a parsnip.

"Oh, that's normal," said Wendell.

"Hold these," the knight said to Christiana, thrusting chicken and parsnip through the bars.

Christiana took them both.

"Up," said the knight. "Under your chin. Ye-e-e-e-s. Like that."

"Young Lady Vanderpool," said the knight with the plumed helmet, "I am the castellan of Castle Wanderpoll. I am so sorry for the misunderstanding."

"I'll let it go this time," said Christiana, turning her nose up, "provided, of course, that you free my friends."

"I regret that is impossible," said the castellan. "Indeed, for a Wanderpoll to claim friendship with a dragon—well, we have much to discuss. Doubtless this is a misunderstanding. But we would not dream of leaving you in a cell, of course." He gestured, and one of the other knights hurried to unlock the cell.

Christiana paused on the threshold and shot an agonized glance back at Danny and Wendell. Then she straightened and lifted her chin.

WHAT OF THE IGUANA? HE'S MY LACKEY.

". . . we'll discuss it," said the castellan, slamming the cell door. The knights closed around her in an honor guard, and Christiana swept out of the hallway as if she owned it.

The clanking footsteps receded and left Danny and Wendell alone in the silence of the dungeon.

FIRE!

Sitting in the cell without Christiana was, if possible, even more boring than sitting in a cell with her. The only difference was that you could fart loudly and not get a lecture about barbarism and the fall of Western civilization.

There was a bucket of water in the corner. Danny was so thirsty he took a drink, but it tasted like there was something growing in it.

"So what's a lackey?" asked Danny.

"A servant," said Wendell. "Only worse. Um. Kinda like how Frankie the chameleon follows Big Eddy around, you know?"

"Oh." Danny thought for a minute. "Okay. What's a castellan?"

"The person in charge of a castle. Not like the king, but like . . . um . . . a sheriff. From the Latin *castellanus,* derived from—"

"That's okay," said Danny hurriedly. Once Wendell went to Latin, you had to shake him to get him to talk like a normal person again.

They sat in silence. Danny picked at the straw.

"What do you think she's doing?" asked Wendell.

"I hope she's finding Spencer."

AND NOT STUCK ON A LIBRARY WALL SOMEWHERE. SERIOUSLY, WHO DOES THAT?

"Didn't your granddad used to roast knights?" asked Wendell. "When we saw him that one time, he kept telling you to go slay some knights."

"Well, he *said* he did." Danny scowled. "I don't know. I think it was more of a thing back in the day. And he didn't stick them on the wall of his cottage. That would just be *weird*."

SO KNIGHTS AND DRAGONS DON'T SLAY EACH OTHER ANYMORE?

I DON'T THINK THERE'S ENOUGH OF US LEFT. BESIDES, YOU CAN'T JUST GO AROUND SLAYING PEOPLE. NOT FOR REAL.

Danny groaned. One thing for sure, if Spencer got slain, Danny's aunt was going to freak out. He might not be a very good son (in Danny's opinion), but she liked him alive. If Danny showed up without Spencer—or worse yet, with Spencer's head on a plaque—

Oh, that'd be bad.

"You're leaking smoke again," said Wendell.

"Sorry." Danny eyed the bars. "Maybe we could melt our way out!"

"There is no way that's a good idea."

"No, it totally is! I'll breathe fire on the bars and get them red hot and then they'll melt, and—"

"Well, it depends on the exact alloy, but at *least* 2,500 degrees!"

Danny had to admit that sounded pretty hot. Still, his fire was pretty hot, wasn't it? He was so worried about Spencer that he could feel the fire lurking in the back of his throat. He felt like a commercial for acid reflux medication.

It sure *felt* hot.

"Say something to make me mad," he told Wendell.

"What?"

"So I can breathe fire! Make me mad!"

"I . . . uh . . . um . . . your mother wears army boots?"

Danny rolled his eyes. "Better than that! And Mom's boots are awesome! She could kick a door down with those things!"

ERR . . . UM . . . YOU'RE STUPID AND YOU CAN'T BREATHE FIRE?

Danny sighed. If anything, Wendell's attempts to help were making him *less* mad.

"Oh!" said the iguana. "I know! Heads on the library wall! Dragon heads! I bet they have glass eyeballs! *I bet they use them for coat racks!*"

The bars didn't melt. They did turn a dull reddish color, but they didn't get runny.

"Told you," said Wendell.

"I'm just getting warmed up." Danny took a deep breath. The bars made little *ping!ping!ping!* noises as they cooled.

"Uh—"

FWOOOM! Danny exhaled over the bars again.

They were so hot now that it was uncomfortable to stand next to them, but they still didn't melt. Wendell retreated to the far side of the cell.

"Uh, Danny—"

"Relax. I can totally do it! They're much redder this time!"

"Danny—"

"Third time's bound to be the charm—"

"Whoops."

Danny hurriedly choked back the fire and began stomping on the burning straw. Whatever the melting point of steel was, apparently the *burning* point of straw was a lot lower.

Unfortunately, stomping on the straw made bits of it fly into the air. Where they landed, new flames sprang up.

"Hrrggkk . . . hgg . . . Danny . . . !"

Smoke billowed out of the cell. Wendell began coughing wretchedly. Danny did a little better, since dragons are used to smoke, but it was still getting awfully thick. He put an arm over his face and kicked over the bucket of water in the corner. It sloshed across the floor and put the fire out with a wet hiss.

Nearly half the straw had turned black and curled up. The cell looked like the floor was covered in dead spiders. Danny pushed it away from the wall, looking for stray embers . . . and stopped.

"Hrrghk . . . hrkk . . . huh?"

"Come over here! I think there's a hole in the wall! The straw was covering it up!"

Sure enough, there was a narrow crack in the wall where the mortar between two stones had crumbled away. It was so thin that the knights might not have bothered to patch it up, if they'd even noticed it. After all, no grown-up could possibly fit through a hole that size . . .

OH, RELAX.

THIS ONE JUST GOES TO THE CELL NEXT TO US. LOOK, YOU CAN STICK YOUR ARM RIGHT THROUGH IT.

"We won't fit," said Wendell practically.

"If we could get one more brick out . . ."

The same thought struck both of them simultaneously.

"I wonder if the other cell is locked . . . ?"

Danny had his head halfway into the hole when he heard the door opening.

The knights were back.

LADY WANDERPOLL STRIKES

Wendell grabbed him around the waist and hauled backward. Danny flattened himself against the wall to hide the crack from view.

The knights marched in.

"Whew!" said one, waving his hand through the smoke. "What happened in here?"

"Uh . . ." Danny and Wendell exchanged glances. The knights must know that dragons could breathe fire, but did they know *Danny* could breathe fire?

"Spontaneous combustion?" said Wendell. "It just . . . err . . . caught fire. Suddenly."

The knight rolled his eyes. "Yeah, right. Typical dragon behavior," he said. "You get frustrated and you start setting everything on fire. Sheesh."

"Never mind that," said Danny. "Where's Christiana?"

The knights grinned. A short figure pushed past them and came up to the bars.

"Ahem," said Christiana.

"I have seen the truth!" cried Christiana, waving her arms in the air. "They have shown me the Great Book of Wanderpoll, and traced my lineage back to the first knights of the realm! The blood of a thousand dragon-slayers runs in my veins!"

"That is so not cool!" said Danny.

"Knights and dragons can never be friends! In a few hours, your worthless cousin shall be slain, to prove the worthiness of the youngest scion of House Wanderpoll."

"Wait, what?" Danny almost lunged for the bars, but remembered just in time to keep his back to the wall. "They're going to slay Spencer?!"

"This very evening!" said Christiana. "As is only right! In the amphitheater in the center of the castle. And there is nothing you can do about it, dragon, for your cousin is held atop the tallest tower, and you are trapped down here in the entirely escape-proof dungeon!"

. . . MOSTLY ESCAPE-PROOF. I MEAN, IT DOESN'T COME UP MUCH.

"Totally escape-proof!" shouted Christiana. "Nobody is escaping! I mean, with guards patrolling the far end of the hallway and the only windows looking directly over the moat, how could anyone escape?"

"It's a pretty good dungeon," admitted the knight.

Danny was furious. How dare Christiana throw them over for the knights? Didn't their friendship mean anything? Hadn't they faced ghosts and fairies and toxic mutant pack rats together?

He couldn't breathe fire on her—it was Christiana!—but he kinda wished he was close enough to the bars to hock a loogie.

"I shall take my leave of you—forever!" said Christiana, putting the back of her hand to her forehead. "But you, Wendell—you're not a dragon. I only pity you for being associated with such scaly scum. Give me your hand in friendship before I go."

"Good-bye forever!" said Christiana. "I'm off to be fitted for armor and become a knight!"

"I hope you get armor rash!" yelled Danny.

"Uh . . . huh . . . hmm . . . bye, Christiana," said Wendell.

The knights clanked away, taking their former friend. Danny heard the hall door slam, and the sound of a key turning in the lock.

He sagged away from the crack in the wall.

He ran out of breath and had to take another one. Smoke started to drift out his nose again. "Dragons don't stink! And what's a flatworm, anyway?"

Wendell rubbed his forehead. "It's a little slimy thing that wiggles around in the mud. And you're an idiot."

Danny blinked at him.

"Christiana was *acting*," said Wendell. "Jeez, she was like someone in a bad commercial. And she managed to tell us where Spencer's being held, where the guards are, and what they plan to do with him."

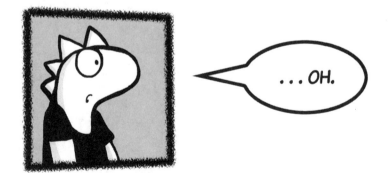

SQUELCH!

The key didn't fit the cell door. "She probably couldn't get to the key for our cell," said Wendell practically. "I bet the knights were keeping a really close eye on that one. She probably figured we could get out of the cell on our own."

"If this is the hall key, it's good enough," said Danny, who was feeling guilty that he'd suspected Christiana of turning on them. He should have known better.

Although that bit about being lower than flatworms still rankled, and seriously, *vileness upon the earth?* That sounded *really* insulting. And also weirdly formal, but then again, it *was* Christiana.

They turned back to the crack in the wall. The mortar was soft and crumbled when Danny banged on it with the wooden bucket.

"Oh, good," said Wendell. "This should only take hours and hours."

"It's not that bad," said Danny. "Don't you remember that report I did on Alcatraz?"

"Of course I do," said Wendell. "It's the only one you've ever gotten an A plus on. I think your mom framed it."

"Yeah! When those prisoners dug their way out of Alcatraz, all they had were spoons! We've got a *bucket!*"

In the end, it took about half an hour. The bucket did not survive the experience, but once it had fallen apart, the metal ring that went around the wooden slats came in handy. Danny braced it around the edge of the brick and pulled.

CHuNk!

The brick popped free. The resulting hole was just large enough for a dragon to fit through—and Wendell, if he took off his glasses.

Once they'd squeezed through the crack in the wall, the other cell door was unlocked. They tiptoed to the end of the hall and Wendell put his key in the hallway door.

KA-CHUNK!

It turned. They both let out a deep breath.

"There's gonna be a guard at the end of the hallway," whispered Wendell. Danny nodded.

They eased the door open a crack and peered around the edge. There was a short flight of stairs, leading to an elevated hall. Watery light streamed through the windows and danced on the ceiling.

They crept partway up the stairs and peered over the top.

The hall was lined with suits of armor. Wendell let out a squeak and ducked back below the top stair.

Danny elbowed him in the ribs. "Dummy! They're only suits!"

"What if one of them's real?" whispered Wendell, elbowing him back.

"Then he's got no legs!"

. . . OH.

At the far end, past the empty suits of armor, Danny could see another hallway at right angles to this one. There was no door between the two.

"I don't see anybody—" he began.

Wendell grabbed his arm. "Wait! *Listen!*"

Danny cocked his head. Wendell held his breath.

Then he heard it.

CLANK
CLANK
CLANK
CLANK
CLANK
CLANK

A knight passed by the end of the hallway. They could hear the rattle of his armor receding as he walked away. *Clank . . . clank . . . clank . . .*

"Now!" whispered Danny.

They lunged from hiding toward the nearest window.

There was a pair of iron bars set into it, too close to squeeze through. Danny growled with frustration.

THAT ONE!
DOWN AT THE END!
IT'S MISSING
A BAR!

"Great!" said Danny. "I'll stand on your shoulders—"

"You *always* stand on my shoulders," said the iguana. "I want to be the one who stands on somebody's shoulders for a change!"

"Oh my god, Wendell, is this really the time to talk about this?!"

Wendell folded his arms. "Well, I've been meaning to say something. All this can't be good for my back. Seriously, I'm gonna be the first person in history who needs a chiropractor before they're out of middle school."

"Fine! You stand on *my* shoulders! Just hurry up!"

"It's the moat," Wendell reported.

"Well, duh!"

"There's nowhere to stand. We'd fall into the moat."

"Uh-huh," said Danny, listening. Had that been a distant clank?

"Maybe there's another way out—"

It had definitely been a clank.

"Hurry!" hissed Danny. "Pull me up!"

"But we'll both fall in the moat!"

Clank . . . clank . . .

"That's the point! The moat is out there! The dungeon's in here! If we're in the moat, we're not in the dungeon!"

"But the moat is disgusting!"

Clank . . .

"If we don't get out of here, they're going to slay Spencer!"

Wendell crawled halfway through the window and stopped.

CLANK . . .

IT'S NOT THAT I'M NOT OPPOSED TO THEM SLAYING SPENCER—IN THEORY—BUT I DON'T KNOW IF MY SENSE OF OBLIGATION TO YOUR COUSIN EXCEEDS MY SENSE OF ALL THAT SLIME.

CLANK
   CLANK
      CLANK

The knight was nearly at the end of the hallway. Another few seconds, and he'd see Danny standing only a few feet away. Even if the last suit of armor hid most of him, there was still the problem of his feet, which would be clearly visible below the edge of the armor.

Danny jumped for the wall, grabbed the rough edge of a stone with his fingertips, and clung.

Wendell dropped down the outside of the wall, clinging to the last bar with both hands.

They held their breath.

CLANK

Was the knight stopping?

There was an agonizing pause. Danny's fingertips burned. In another second, he was going to fall to the floor, and there was no way the knight could miss him—

CLANK

CLANK

CLANK

Danny leaned against the wall, weak-kneed with relief.

Wendell poked his head back through the window. "Are you okay?"

"I'm fine," said Danny. "But he's going to come back from the other direction, and there's no way he won't see us from that angle."

"I'm going to need antibiotics," said Wendell. "This moat is *nasty.*"

WHEN WE GET HOME, I WILL GET YOU ALL THE ANTIBIOTICS YOU WANT! JUST PULL ME UP!

Wendell leaned down and hauled him up.

The iguana had been right. There really was nowhere to stand. Wendell hung on to the bar and Danny perched in the window, looking down into the murky green depths of the moat.

"I don't wanna swim in that," said Wendell.

Danny had to admit, once he was up close and personal, he didn't really want to swim in it either. The moat was *nasty*. Parts of it looked almost solid with scum.

"It's no worse than the Sargasso Sea," he said, not very convincingly.

". . . riiiiight," said Wendell.

Danny twisted to look up. They were about twenty feet from the drawbridge. The walls were slick with moss. They didn't look very climbable.

"We have to get around to the tower," he said. "But we'll have to find another way in."

"Maybe you could find it and come back and tell me," said Wendell. "I'll wait."

Danny heard a distant clanking sound.

"Unless you want to wait inside the cell, I think we better go!" he said. "Before they wonder what the splashing is!"

He took a deep breath, wriggled through the window—and dove into the moat.

The water was warm and sticky.

Really sticky.

Danny had never before contemplated what it would be like to swim in a giant booger. It couldn't be much worse than the moat.

There was a splash—more of a *splorch*!—and Wendell landed next to him.

Moving in the water wasn't quite like swimming. You didn't sink. It was so thick and slimy that you just floundered on the surface.

Danny squelched toward the drawbridge. He didn't know if there were any knights about, but if so, he wanted to be able to hide under the drawbridge while they passed. Wendell flailed after him. The surface of the moat squelched closed behind them.

"It's not like it's *just* slime," said Danny. "It's got layers and everything."

The sludge around his legs felt like mud, then there was a layer that felt almost like tapioca pudding. His stomach was in something watery, and a green skin of algae was sticking to his armpits.

"I am getting new and exciting diseases," moaned Wendell.

They reached the underside of the drawbridge. Big stone pilings held up the castle side of the bridge. There was just enough of a ledge to crawl up on.

The iguana looked miserable. There was duck-weed stuck all over him, like green measles. He tried to clean his glasses on his shirt, but they only got slimier. "I think we should go home and get some grown-ups."

Danny shook his head. "We might not get back in time to save Spencer."

Wendell groaned. "Danny, if it was you, that'd be one thing, but I'm not sure your cousin's *worth* it."

"We don't have any choice," said Danny. "Look, he annoys me too—you think I like having somebody go *wa-waaaaah* . . . every time I lose a life on a video game?—but still. He may not be much, but he's family."

He didn't always like Spencer, but leaving him in a castle where they stuck dragon heads on the walls—no. Just no. Danny Dragonbreath had his limits. He was going to get to Spencer if he had to climb up the outside of the tower by himself.

MEETING MR. SCOWLY

"You can't climb up the outside of the tower by yourself," said Wendell.

"Are you gonna come with me?" asked Danny. "You said yourself that Spencer wasn't worth it."

The iguana shook his head slowly. "I dunno. But if you go yourself, *you* might get caught, and then I'd have to try and rescue you, and I'm not good at daring single-handed rescues."

Danny hid a grin. "Well, maybe not. But I bet you could write an awesome paper about it."

"Best bibliography in town," said Wendell.

The two reptiles gazed up the tower wall. From underneath the drawbridge, they had swum (more or less) to the tower.

Maybe it was just the angle, but it looked a lot taller from down here.

It was nearly dark, but Danny could make out the shape of stones in the wall.

"I think we can climb it," he said. "It looks old."

"Yeah . . ." said Wendell. "Then we just need some way up from the moat."

HOW 'BOUT THIS RAIN GUTTER?

"I guess even castles need rain gutters," said Wendell.

"After all, I bet if the basement here floods, it *really* floods."

The rainspout got them up on the roof. The stones were so large and the mortar so old that once they were past the ring of slime from the moat, it wasn't much harder than climbing a ladder.

I'M DYING! I'VE BEEN CLIMBING FOR HOURS! I'M GOING TO FALL OFF!

Danny pulled himself up the last few feet and fell over the top of the battlements. He'd been afraid that some knights might be patrolling them, but apparently they'd all gone inside for dinner or something.

Wendell, alas, did not have it quite so easy.

"Dude," said Danny. "You've gone three feet. It's way easier than climbing the ropes in gym."

"Do you *remember* the last time we did the ropes in gym?"

. . . UM . . .
GOOD EFFORT,
WENDELL . . . ?

It would have been really dark, but the knights of Castle Wanderpoll were apparently quite modern in some regards, and there were lights flanking the drawbridge and the driveway. They cast an eerie orange glow from below.

Eventually Wendell crawled to within a few feet of the top, and Danny pulled him up and over. The iguana sagged against the battlements. "That was awful," he said.

"Come on, that was nothing. You couldn't have fallen if you wanted to. You could have taken a nap on some of those ledges."

A pair of headlights flashed into view. Danny and Wendell flattened themselves behind the ramparts.

The car wound its way up the drive and parked in front of the castle. They heard a door slam, and then the creak of footsteps across the draw-bridge.

"I guess somebody just came home?" said Wendell.

"Yeah—or they're getting an audience together to watch a knight skewer Spencer."

They hurried along the battlements to the tower, keeping low in case any more cars came. At the base of the tower, they looked up.

"Shouldn't be hard to climb," said Danny. "There are even gargoyles to grab on to if we need it."

"It looks different from up here," said Wendell.

Y'KNOW . . . MORE IMMEDIATE. AND TALLER. DEFINITELY TALLER.

"You'll be fine," said Danny. "Just don't look down."

"Why does everyone always say that?" asked Wendell. "It doesn't matter if I *look* down or not. I'm *thinking* about down!"

FINE, THEN DON'T THINK DOWN.

NOT HELPING.

HEY, WHAT'S THAT? I THINK I SEE—

—SOMETHING.

"Well," said Wendell, "I guess that means we're on the right track."

They kept climbing. The stones had slimy patches that skidded under their fingers. Wendell yelped whenever he encountered one.

They were almost halfway up the tower when there was a crunch of gravel and headlights swung into the driveway.

"More cars!" hissed Danny. "Quick, go around the back!"

The headlights washed over them and moved on. Danny and Wendell waited, not daring to move. The slam of the car door seemed very far away.

The drawbridge door opened. There weren't any loud voices or alarms. Danny relaxed. Wendell sagged. Fluffy cooed.

A breeze started up. This was refreshing for about the first five seconds, and then Danny started to worry it would blow them off the tower. The pigeon flapped its wings for balance.

Wendell let out a terrified meeping noise and wrapped his arms around the nearest gargoyle.

"Come on, Wendell!" said Danny. "We're nearly at the top!"

"That only means we're *really, really* far from the bottom!"

"You can't just stay there," said Danny. "I mean, I suppose you *can,* but we don't have much time to save Spencer—"

"You go save Spencer," said Wendell, eyes tightly shut. "I will stay with the gargoyle. I will name him Mister Scowly and we will be friends."

"But how are we going to get you down?"

"When you've saved Spencer, get the fire department to bring out a ladder."

Danny rubbed his forehead with his free hand. "Seriously?"

Wendell clung more tightly to Mister Scowly.

"What happens when you have to go to the bathroom?"

The iguana opened one eye. "Oh. Hmm."

"Dude, the window is five feet from here."

The breeze whipped around them. Wendell sighed from the bottom of his toes.

"It better only be five feet," he muttered.

"Four and a half, tops."

"Good-bye, Mister Scowly. I'll always treasure our time together."

It was more like six feet, but Wendell's vision wasn't that great, even with his glasses. Danny climbed into the tower window and reached down to pull Wendell up.

Wendell rolled over the edge and sank down onto the floor, dripping moat slime all over the carpet. Fluffy took off, flapping around the room and cooing excitedly.

. . . DANNY?

THE UNWANTED RESCUE

"I'm getting some mixed signals here," said Danny.

Actually, he was a bit miffed. He'd just escaped from a dungeon, swum a moat, and climbed a tower, all because Spencer had sent him a note saying he was in trouble—and his cousin didn't seem very happy to see him.

Now that he looked around the tower, it was a lot nicer than the dungeon too. Spencer had a bed and a TV—with a video game system, no less! In fact, it looked like he'd been in the middle of a game when they came in the window!

"Didn't you send me that letter?" asked Danny. "By pigeon? That you were *kidnapped*?"

"Well, yeah," said Spencer. "I mean, Fluffy was living up here anyway, on the window ledge, and he was really nice and I drew him a little picture of you—"

"It's okay," said Danny hurriedly, not wanting to be exposed to Spencer's art.

"It's really cool! You're trying to breathe fire and you can't and Wendell's pointing at you and there's one of the alien tripods from *Night of the Living Tripod 4* in the background—"

"Anyway," said Spencer, "when Fluffy came back, I thought maybe you weren't coming, or had gotten lost or grounded or something."

"I wasn't just gonna let you get kidnapped by knights," said Danny, annoyed. "How did that happen, anyway?"

"Oh," said Spencer. "See, I made this friend at after-school care—his name's Freddy, and he's a knight!"

"He totally understands what it's like to be semi-mythical!" said Spencer. "He is too! It's awesome! And his mom's super-nice. Only I came over for a sleepover, and his granddad realized I was a dragon, and . . . well . . ."

"He kidnapped you," said Danny grimly. "Are you sure that wasn't this Freddy kid's plan all along?"

"No!" said Spencer. "He's my friend! And his mom's an environmentalist!"

"Oh," said Spencer. "Well, see, *Freddy's* still my friend—but his granddad's really scary! I mean, it was fine at first, because we were having popcorn and watching a *Fists of Newt-Addled Fury* marathon, but then his granddad saw me and wanted to put me in the dungeon—he's super-old and super-strict, and he was saying all these things about, I don't know, traditions and knights and something stupid like that—and then Freddy's sister convinced them to just put me up here in the tower, not the dungeon, she's super-nice, even if she's kind of a know-it-all—but then I talked to Freddy and he had an idea—I had already sent you the note, though, after I got locked in the tower, but before I talked to Freddy—"

Danny's eyes were starting to glaze over. He pulled himself together. "His sister locked you in the tower?!"

"Only because it wasn't the dungeon! They don't have cable in the dungeon or anything!"

"Do you know they have *dragon heads* in the library here?!"

Spencer's eyes went wide. "No way! Freddy never said anything about *that!*"

Danny sighed. "Look. Knights . . . knights are bad news. We have to get out of here. We can go back out the window—maybe if we knot the bedsheets together—"

BUT I CAN'T LEAVE YET—

There was a distant thudding as a door opened and closed somewhere at the base of the tower.

"Oh no!" said Spencer. "The knights are coming! Quick, you two, hide!"

Wendell dove under the bed. Danny sputtered.

"But—we're here to rescue you! We need to leave right now!"

"Later!" said Spencer. "If they find you, it'll ruin everything!"

Danny might have argued further, but Spencer's face was starting to screw up and turn red the way that indicated he was about to have a serious tantrum. Danny would almost rather face knights. He crawled under the bed next to Wendell.

Spencer picked up the video game controller and turned his back to the door.

The door opened. The castellan—the knight with the big plumy helmet who seemed to be in charge—came in. "Dragon!" he boomed. "It is time to end your foul life!"

"Okay," said Spencer, sounding bored. "Just let me save my game."

He clicked a few buttons, then scrambled to his feet.

The knight swept Danny's cousin out of the room, not bothering to close the door behind them.

Danny waited until he heard the door at the bottom of the tower slam, then climbed out from under the bed.

"We have to follow them! They're going to slay him!"

HE DIDN'T ACTUALLY SEEM THAT WORRIED ABOUT IT.

THAT'S
'CAUSE HE'S
AN IDIOT!

"I don't think he even knows what slaying means! He probably thinks they throw you a party or something!"

Wendell rubbed the back of his neck. "Didn't he watch you play *Monster Slayer IV: Battle for the Chimera Throne*? That was like wall-to-wall slaying."

"Yeah, well, he was too busy telling me about how his friend played it faster and better and had all the cheat codes. Come on! This Freddy kid's obviously convinced him it's going to be okay when it's not. We've got to save him!"

COO!

Sneaking through the inside of the castle was, if possible, even more nerve-wracking than sneaking up the outside. On the one hand, there was a chance of guards around every corner, hardly anywhere to run, and the possibility of unexpectedly locked doors.

On the other hand, your arms didn't get as tired and there wasn't nearly as much wind.

The castle looked like you'd expect a castle to look, full of tapestries and long winding carpets and flagstone floors and big iron candlesticks.

Well . . . mostly.

What Danny hadn't expected to find in a medieval castle were quite so many *posters.*

They weren't bad posters. Most of them were of sad-eyed baby seals, and some of them were of the planet earth with a faucet on it, and little educational notes about how many gallons of water got wasted every day watering the lawn.

"This one's outdated," whispered Wendell. "They banned DDT years ago. Pelican populations have bounced back wonderfully."

"Uh-huh," said Danny.

"It was supposed to kill bugs. But it made the pelican eggshells super-thin, so they were laying, like, scrambled eggs."

"That's tragic," said Danny. "I feel terrible for them. I will go and hug a pelican as soon as we're out of here. In the meantime, do you think maybe we could, I don't know, *find my cousin before somebody shoves a lance through him!?*"

"You don't have to get all snitty about it . . ."

They snuck down another hallway. It had three suits of armor, an iron maiden, and a very depressing poster about the Amazon rainforest.

"What are you talking about? There were all those knights!"

"Maybe," said Wendell dubiously. "But I'm starting to wonder if there aren't that many knights. I mean, how many have we actually *seen?*"

"Um," said Danny. "There were three who dragged us in, plus the castellan. Plus this Freddy kid and his sister."

"That's four and two halves," said Wendell. "That's really not a lot of knights for a place this size. And have you noticed how run-down everything looks? The carpet's worn through here and the wallpaper in that last room looked older than my mom."

"There could be a lot more knights that we don't know about," said Danny. "Dozens. Hundreds! Anyway, they all look alike in the armor. We've only seen like four in one place."

"You're the one always saying knights are an endangered species . . ."

YEAH,
AND THEY'RE
GONNA BE A LOT MORE
ENDANGERED IF THEY
HURT SPENCER!

Still, it was starting to seem like Wendell might be right. They crept from shadow to shadow, doorway to doorway, poster to poster . . . and didn't see a single knight.

"Maybe they're all at the arena," said Danny grimly. "Watching Spencer get slain."

"But where's the arena?"

With a flutter of wings and a worried coo, Fluffy settled atop a nearby statue.

"Fluffy!" said Danny. "I wondered where you'd got off to!"

"I suppose he'll come in handy if we're attacked by corn," said Wendell.

"Pfff. I'll ask him where the arena is."

"Their brains are the size of a cashew . . ." said Wendell, not quite under his breath.

"Don't listen to him, Fluffy," said Danny. "You're a great pigeon."

NOW FLUFFY, LISTEN CLOSELY. DO YOU KNOW WHERE THE ARENA IS?

COO!

YOU KNOW MY COUSIN SPENCER? HE'S AT THE ARENA, AND WE NEED TO GET TO HIM BEFORE SOMETHING BAD HAPPENS.

Coo!

The pigeon fluttered to Danny's head and extended a wing. "Coo-oo—OO!"

"Thataway!" said Danny.

"Thanks," said Wendell, "I could probably have figured that one out, even without awesome rat-speaking powers."

Dragon, iguana, and pigeon took off at a jog.

Fluffy directed them through a long hallway, down a flight of stairs, and through another set of doors.

"It just occurred to me," said Wendell, "that if we go tearing into the arena, all the knights are going to be there."

"Uh-huh," said Danny. "Your point?"

I DUNNO, MAYBE THERE'S A MORE STRATEGIC WAY TO DO IT?

"Like, a way that doesn't get us immediately re-captured?"

Danny had to admit that the iguana was onto something. "Right. More reconnaissance. And no, I'm not going to spell it."

He looked up at the pigeon.

FLUFFY, IS THERE A WINDOW OR SOMETHING WE CAN LOOK IN, RATHER THAN PLOWING RIGHT INTO THE ARENA?

Fluffy thought for a minute. "Coo!"

They went back through the doors and up a shallower flight of stairs. There was a closed door at the end of the hall, next to a poster of a sad-looking rhinoceros.

". . . Coo . . ." said Fluffy, in what, for a pigeon, was probably a whisper.

Danny and Wendell approached the door and Danny leaned his head against it, listening.

"Crowd noises," he reported to Wendell.

Wendell nodded.

Danny reached for the doorknob and eased the door open.

DIE, FOUL DRAGON!

The door led to a narrow balcony. The seats were empty. Danny tiptoed to the edge and looked down.

It was the arena.

Honestly, when Danny heard the word "arena" he thought . . . big. Amphitheater big. Hockey arena–sized, at least. Lights! Big video monitors with instant replay! Rows of seats that went up so high that you got altitude sickness!

The arena in Castle Wanderpoll was a small sawdust circle, about the size of the little rings

where people show farm animals at the county fair. It had a low wall and two doors opening into it. There were three rows of seats in a circle around the railing, slightly raised, and the balcony had another two rows. (Actually, parts of the balcony didn't even have that. Somebody had taken out the seats on the side opposite Danny and was using it to store some boxes and an old pool table.) There were banners with the familiar parsnip-and-chicken, but they looked old and faded and at least one had been a bedsheet in a former life.

It was . . . well, pretty dinky, actually. And it looked like Wendell had been right, because there were only four knights in the audience, and another very small knight in the middle of the arena.

"Do you see Spencer?" whispered Wendell.

Danny shook his head. "They can't have slain him already—they didn't have time!"

"The one in the arena," said Wendell. "That must be Freddy?"

Danny studied the small knight. "He's awfully

small," he said slowly. "And he's having a lot of trouble lifting his sword. I don't know if he *could* slay Spencer."

"Just 'cause you're small doesn't mean you're not fierce," said Wendell. "I mean, piranhas are small! And shrews. And rabid lemmings."

"I wish we had some rabid lemmings," Danny sighed. "They'd be a great distraction for the knights." (He could actually see a number of uses for rabid lemmings in everyday life, but this didn't seem like the time to get into it.)

IT SLICES! IT DICES!
IT WILL DISRUPT STANDARDIZED
TESTING IN FOUR SECONDS FLAT!

"There must be at least one more knight some-where," whispered Wendell. "And Christiana should be here somewhere too . . ."

The castellan was one of the four. He stood up and spread his hands.

BROTHERS! WE ARE HERE TODAY TO WITNESS MY GRANDSON FREDERICK'S INVESTITURE AS A FULL KNIGHT OF WANDERPOLL!

Danny leaned over. "Say, Wendell—"

"People get *invested* with an office or a rank," said Wendell. "That's why judges say 'By the power i*nvested* in me.' The act of investing Freddy is his investiture."

"If the nerd thing doesn't work out, you have a future writing vocabulary quizzes."

"Our old traditions have gone un-honored for too long!" cried Freddy's grandfather. "Too many of our sons and daughters have never slain a dragon. But one more Wanderpoll shall stand forth to face the foe! *Release the dragon!*"

Danny stopped worrying about vocabulary.

One of the doors leading to the arena opened. Danny caught a glimpse of a knight behind the door, and then—

Spencer stumbled out into the arena. The small knight in the middle lifted his sword (not without difficulty).

"Let the battle commence!" cried the castellan. "Let Sir Frederick prove himself worthy of knighthood!"

He sat down with a jangling thump.

Spencer looked at Freddy.

Freddy looked at Spencer.

Danny put a hand over his face in sheer embarrassment.

"This is not going to go down as one of history's great battles," said Wendell.

The two combatants circled each other. Freddy couldn't turn very fast because his sword was too heavy for him, so Spencer slowed down to match.

"So that's why he didn't want us to interfere," said Danny. "He and Freddy set it up. It's a *fake* fight."

Spencer charged. The crowd (what there was of it) roared. Freddy quickly realized that he couldn't do anything useful with his sword, dropped it, and prepared to take Danny's cousin on barehanded.

Wendell put his hand over his mouth and tried to stifle hysterical laughter.

"This is horrible," said Danny. "Either one of them is going to trip on the stupid sword and cut himself, or the knights are going to send somebody in to finish the job."

"You think so?"

In the arena, Spencer and Freddy rolled around on the ground. Freddy managed to get on top and sat on the small dragon's chest.

"Um—um—I have you now!"

Danny tensed. Wendell bit the side of his hand to keep from laughing.

"You'll never slay me!" yelled Spencer.

"I've got—um—a sword! Somewhere!" Freddy went for the sword.

He actually had to climb off Spencer to get to the sword. Spencer waited politely on the ground.

"And now, with this sword, I'll slay you, you—you—nasty dragon, you!" shouted Freddy, raising the sword over his head.

The point of the sword wobbled downward.

"Aaaargh!" cried Spencer. He stood up so that he could dramatically fall again.

YOU'VE SLAIN ME!

For a minute, Danny thought they were going to pull it off. It was a stupid fight, but maybe the knights didn't know any better.

But there was a long, awkward silence . . . and then the castellan stood up and said, "Now cut its head off!"

Wendell stopped laughing.

Danny swung over the railing, hung from it briefly, and dropped to the last row of chairs below.

He vaulted over the railing around the arena and ran toward the fallen Spencer. It looked like the sword was sticking straight up out of his chest.

Freddy, his eyes very wide, fell back. He ran for the far side of the arena.

"Spencer!" hissed Danny, feeling a hot, fiery pressure in his throat. "Spencer, get up!" He dropped to his knees. "If you get your head cut off, your mom is gonna kill me!"

"Go away!" whispered Spencer out of the side of his mouth. "You're ruining everything!"

"Say what now?"

"It's a fake! He's pretending to slay me so I can get out of here! We worked it all out with his sister—oh—except for the head-chopping bit, we didn't think of that—"

I *TOLD YOU* YOU'D RUIN IT!

"Fetch the Lady Christiana!" he cried. "This is a foe more suited to her size! Let *her* earn her knighthood as well!"

DRAGON VS. KNIGHT

The door to the arena opened. A figure in full armor clomped out, and unlike Freddy, she didn't have any trouble carrying her sword.

Danny was pretty sure that Christiana would not actually try to stab him with a sword. Sure, she'd said some pretty insulting things, but Wendell had said it was acting, and Wendell was usually right about that sort of thing.

Plus, they were buddies! Danny would have had a hard time stabbing anybody with a sword— I mean, really doing it, in real life—let alone a good friend. They'd braved pack rats and fairies and jackalope smugglers together! They might not have a perfect friendship, but he and Christiana totally had each other's backs.

This certainty lasted right up to the point where Christiana lowered her sword and charged at him.

UH, CHRISTIANA . . . ?

"Yerrkk!" said Danny, and dove out of the way.

He hit the sawdust floor of the arena and rolled. Christiana swung her sword at him. She missed by a mile, but there was a nasty little whistle as the blade sliced through the air.

"Christiana!?"

"Die, foul dragon scum!" yelled Christiana.

"But—"

She swung.

He ducked.

Now he was starting to get mad. Again.

CHRISTIANA, WHAT ARE YOU DOING?!

She lowered the sword point until it was facing directly at his chest.

"Christiana—"

"Die, draconic lackwit!"

Danny was pretty sure that was insulting, even without Wendell there to tell him.

"But—"

She charged him.

He closed one eye, took aim, and spat fire at her feet. It wasn't anywhere near enough to burn her, but the puff of smoke looked *awfully* impressive.

(Truth was, he felt horribly guilty about breathing fire even *near* Christiana. His mom would kill him if she ever found out. And "But she was coming at me with a sword!" just wouldn't cut it as an excuse. His mom would probably say: "Then you should have found a grown-up and told *them*," and never mind that all the grown-ups in the area were wearing armor and yelling for his blood.)

The knights were going crazy. Danny caught a glimpse of Wendell in the stands.

The iguana had apparently climbed down without anybody noticing. A knight was elbowing him in the ribs and Wendell was elbowing him back, like two spectators at a soccer game. Fluffy was clinging to Wendell's head, flapping wildly.

Christiana shook herself off, wiped ashes from her face—and charged him.

Again.

"Seriously!?" Danny yelled.

She slammed into him, shoulder first, and drove him back against the arena wall.

The knights leaped to their feet, straining to see the action.

"Come on!" hissed Christiana in his ear. "We have to make it look good!"

"Ah-wuh?" said Danny.

"We're acting! It's an act! Now pretend I'm killing you!" She clouted him over the head with the hilt of the sword.

"OW!" said Danny. He didn't have to pretend very hard—that hurt!

Christiana put him in a headlock. "Foul—capitalist—running dog—" She leaned in. "Once you and Spencer both look slain, Freddy's sister will come in to help clean up. She's super-nice, she'll help us escape."

"But she's a knight!" Danny pretended to struggle. Christiana's headlocks were better than Wendell's, but he was mostly worried about the sword, which was perilously close to his face.

"Yeah, well, she's also the one who gave me the key!"

YOU CAN'T WIN, DRAGON!

THEY'RE NOT ALL BAD. I THINK IT'S JUST THE CASTELLAN.

BUT THEY HAVE DRAGON HEADS ON THE LIBRARY WALL!

"They're fiberglass," Christiana said. "I checked. Far as I can tell, they haven't seen a real dragon out here in years and years."

"Really?"

"Yeah."

"But they wanted to cut Spencer's head off!"

"It's mostly the granddad. I think the others just do what he tells them, since Freddy's mom is out of town, and she's the one who stands up to him. Now breathe fire!" she whispered.

"Um . . . I kinda have to be mad . . ." Danny wasn't mad anymore, just very confused.

"Remember that time in third grade when your pants ripped and Big Eddy wrote 'Danny wears Super Skink panties!' on the board?"

I TOLD HIM HOW TO SPELL IT!

Danny took a deep, roaring breath and shot smoke out of his nostrils. Christiana took a step back.

"Why—you—you—
They called me Skinkypants for *days!*" Danny stomped across the arena, breathing fire. The knights were screaming. Christiana retreated, waving her sword.

Even as annoyed as he was about the Super Skink panties incident, Danny was careful not to actually hit Christiana. But if the knights wanted a show—well, they were going to get a *show!*

He flamed. He frothed. He ran at Christiana waving his arms and spouting smoke.

Freddy cowered on one side of the arena, over the "body" of Spencer, who had forgotten he was supposed to be dead and was watching with wide eyes. Fortunately the knights were much too intent on Danny and Christiana to notice.

RAAAAWR!

He flung himself at Christiana, caught her sword under one arm, and threw himself to the ground, kicking wildly.

"I am slain!" he cried. "You've slain me, you—uh—horrible knight of dooooom!"

"Well," said Christiana, "thank goodness that's ov—"

"SLAIN!" screamed Danny, thrashing around on the floor of the arena. "OH THE PAIN!"

"He's dead," said Christiana.

"Everything's . . . getting dark . . ."

"Really *truly* dead," Christiana added, kicking him. "As in the not-talking-anymore kind of dead."

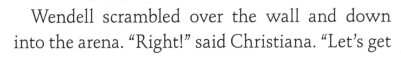

LET ME THROUGH! I'M HER LACKEY!

Wendell scrambled over the wall and down into the arena. "Right!" said Christiana. "Let's get out of here . . ." She raised her voice again. "We shall take them and cut their heads off for the library wall!"

The knights were cheering wildly. Christiana took a bow and then pulled Freddy out into the center of the arena and made him take a bow too.

Meanwhile, another knight had come out of the doorway. She was taller than Freddy, but not by much, and she was chewing gum rather loudly. She and Wendell grabbed Danny by the wrists and ankles and carried him through the door while Christiana and Freddy kept the knights distracted.

The doorway led to a small chamber with benches like a locker room. Danny sat up. "That was awesome!"

Freddy's sister shook her head and laughed. She looked about fifteen years old. "That was quite a performance, kiddo. Even if you hammed up the death scene. Let me go get your cousin . . ." She went out again. A minute later, she and Christiana carried Spencer into the locker, followed by Freddy, followed by Fluffy the pigeon.

"Are you Danny?" asked Freddy. "I mean, I guess you must be . . . Spencer told me all about you!"

"It's fine," said Wendell, making soothing gestures. "You can *both* be endangered species."

Freddy's sister grinned. "Not nearly as endangered as Granddad's gonna be when Mom gets back from her trip and finds out what he's been doing. Kidnapping kids in the middle of a sleepover!" She shook her head in disbelief. "And *endangered* kids! Mom is gonna be *furious*."

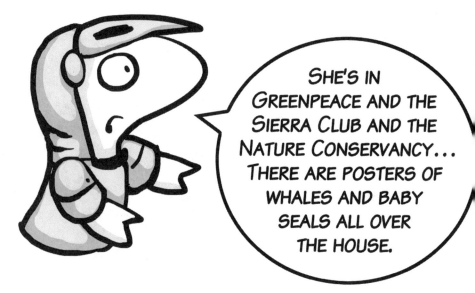

SHE'S IN GREENPEACE AND THE SIERRA CLUB AND THE NATURE CONSERVANCY... THERE ARE POSTERS OF WHALES AND BABY SEALS ALL OVER THE HOUSE.

Freddy stared at his feet. "Granddad's usually not like this—he's pretty nice, most of the time—but he just goes crazy when dragons are involved."

"It's cool," said Danny. "Well, not *cool,* but you know. My grandfather Turlingsward gets really weird about knights too. Although he's never actually kidnapped one." (Privately he thought this was because it would require far too much effort, not because of any great virtue on his grandfather's part.)

"They'd probably get along really well . . . until they tried to slay each other," said Freddy sadly. "Anyway, when Granddad found out that Spencer was a dragon, he got this stupid idea I should slay him to uphold the tradition of dragon-slaying knights. I think he's mad because he never got to slay a dragon himself." He looked up at Danny worriedly. "I'm really sorry, Danny. Spencer and I had it all worked out, so I'd pretend to slay him and Granddad'd be proud of me and everything would go back to normal, but I didn't think you and Christiana would have to fight too."

"Oh, I didn't mind . . ." said Christiana, grinning. "I've wanted to hit Danny with a sword since third grade." She elbowed him in the ribs.

Danny elbowed her back. "Yeah, well . . . we've

still got a score to settle about the Super Skink panties thing." Christiana snickered.

Apparently she hadn't minded having fire breathed at her. It occurred to Danny that if Christiana really and truly believed he was a dragon, life might be a little easier now.

"So now what do we do?" asked Wendell. "Can we just leave?"

"And what stops Freddy's granddad from going after any other dragons he runs across?" Danny added.

"You could press charges," said Christiana. "I mean, that's the usual thing to do when you've been kidnapped."

"We'd have to explain about the dragon thing," said Danny.

"And we'd have to explain about the knight thing," said Freddy.

"Mythical creatures like us survive by keeping a low profile," said Freddy's sister.

"Anyway," she added, "I don't think you have to worry about Granddad. He doesn't get out of the house very much. And I called Mom this morning when I realized what had happened, so she's on her way home. When she gets back tomorrow morning, he'll wish he'd never even heard of dragons."

"There were like three other knights, though," said Danny. "Don't we need to worry about them?"

Both Freddy and his sister laughed.

"Them?" Freddy's sister rolled her eyes. "Those are my cousins. They're super-lazy. They'll do whatever Mom tells them . . . unless they want to move out and get jobs and get their own apartments."

"Yeah, she'll totally tell 'em," said Freddy. He hitched himself up and said, in an angry falsetto, "When you're under my roof, mister, you'll do what I tell you or you can hit the highway!"

"Cousins can be a problem," said Danny, and looked innocent when Spencer gave him a suspicious look.

Honestly, he was just as happy to let another knight handle it. The dragon method of handling knights mostly involved a lot of fire and swords and it would be awfully messy.

"Well," said Freddy's sister, "if that's settled—"

AHEM.

GOOD ENOUGH

"These dragons don't seem to be quite dead," said Freddy's grandfather.

Danny tensed. Wendell said, "Eeep!"

Freddy jumped in front of Spencer. "We had a fight, Granddad, you saw it! Now leave him alone!"

"But the dragons are still alive!"

"And they're going to stay that way!" said Freddy's sister. "She stepped in front of Danny and folded her arms. "Mom is not going to be happy about this!"

"Our traditions are in danger of dying out. We have to do whatever we can to preserve them. Your mother understands that," said the castellan, but Danny thought he sounded worried.

The two knights flanking him certainly were.

"Uh," said one.

"Do we have to tell her?" said the other.

"Oh yeah!" said Freddy. "I'm gonna tell her everything! In fact, I could call her *right now—*"

"And I'll back them up," said Christiana. "Nobody cuts my friend's head off!"

"But in the old days, you had to slay a dragon to become a real knight—"

IT'S NOT THE OLD DAYS ANYMORE! MY GRANDDAD'S ALWAYS TALKING ABOUT SLAYING KNIGHTS TOO, BUT WE DON'T DO THAT BECAUSE IT'S STUPID!

"Actually," said Wendell off-hand, "stylized battles between combatants have replaced actual combat in a number of cultures as genuine bloodshed becomes less and less practical . . ."

"But it's *not* good enough!" said the castellan. "It's fake!"

Freddy drew himself up. "So are the heads in the library! And *I* am the one who just fought a dragon, not you, so as a knight, I technically outrank you, Granddad, because you never fought a dragon! *And I say it's good enough!*"

"So do I!" said Christiana.

"Does the dragon get a vote?" asked Danny. "Because I'm okay with knights and dragons having fake fights. I think it makes a lot more sense, now that we're both endangered species."

The castellan looked to his supporters.

"They're *endangered*?" said one, horrified.

"Oh man, Aunt Olivia is gonna be ticked! You *know* how she feels about endangered species!"

"But—*dragons*—!" Freddy's grandfather said—and made a grab for Spencer.

"Aaauggh!" shouted Danny's cousin, ducking.

"Granddad!" yelled Freddy.

"Our traditions are sacred!" yelled the castellan.

Just then a savage cooing came from above his left eye and Fluffy launched himself at the castellan's head.

"Ack!" cried the castellan, batting at the enraged pigeon. "Get it off! Get it off!"

"*Really,* Granddad?" said Freddy's sister. "You want to slay dragons, and you can't handle a *pigeon?*"

"COO!"

Spencer whistled. "Down, Fluffy! Good pigeon!"

Fluffy settled his feathers, pooped firmly on the castellan's head, and flew back to Spencer.

Freddy's sister turned to the two knights. "Just . . . take him up to his room or something. He's gotten all worked up and he probably needs to take something for his heart. And if you do exactly what I say, maybe I'll forget to tell Mom about how you threw these kids in the dungeon."

"Yes'm," said the knights meekly, and led the castellan, now dripping with pigeon poop, into the castle.

AUAHGHGHH! IT POOPED ON ME!

HOMEWARD BOUND

Freddy jogged down to the bus station with them in the dark. "I'll see you at after-school, right?"

"Sure!" said Spencer. "Maybe next time you can come over to my house, though?"

"That'd probably be a good idea."

"Cool!"

"What are you going to do about your mom?" asked Danny. "I mean, you got kidnapped . . . I know you said not to tell her . . ." (Frankly, he thought this was the only thing Spencer had gotten absolutely right, since Spencer's mom would be freaking out and suing everything in sight, and dragonish secrecy would go out the window.)

"I'll just tell Mom the sleepover ran long," said Spencer. "But . . . um . . ."

Danny waited for it.

CAN I PLEASE KEEP FLUFFY? PRETTY PLEASE WITH SUGAR ON TOP?

"It's a *pigeon,*" said Christiana.

"I know! Isn't he great? Mom's allergic to fur,

but he doesn't have fur! And if she won't let me keep him in the house, he can live in the tree outside and I'll bring him birdseed every day and we'll be best friends!"

Knights and dragons (and one iguana lackey) looked at each other.

"Well . . ."

"I mean . . ."

"It's not like they're endangered . . ."

"I think you should probably plan for him to live in the tree," said Wendell. "But you can always open a window and let him into your room."

"Although I'd housebreak him first," added Christiana.

The bus rumbled up in the dark.

"Oh, don't tell me," said the bus driver grimly. "Another Seeing-Eye Pigeon, right?"

The bus drove off into the darkness. Wendell leaned against the back of one of the seats and prepared to take a nap, since their "sleepover" hadn't involved much sleep.

Danny leaned over the back of Christiana's seat.

"I'm not good at 'cool,'" Christiana said. "I think I need a different wardrobe for that."

"No," said Danny. "You and me. I mean, the fire-breathing, and the swords and all. And I guess even the Super Skink underwear."

"Oh, that. Yeah. We're cool." She made a fist and held it up. It took Danny a second to realize that Christiana (Christiana! Of all people!) was giving him a fist bump.

He gave her a fist bump back.

"So you believe I'm a dragon now?"

"Well, you did breathe fire. So I guess I have to. Or believe I'm crazy." She leaned back against the seat. "And don't think I don't kind of want to dissect you and see how you do it, and write a paper on it."

"I'd rather you didn't," said Danny. "You saw what happens when people find out there are dragons around . . ."

"Mmm. Yeah. There's that. But you've got to remember something . . ."

"I," said Christiana, "am now *officially* a knight."
Danny blinked.

"So you better keep on your toes, Danny Dragonbreath," said Christiana, newly knighted. "I'm a certified dragon slayer. And I know where you live."

Danny rolled his eyes. "I'll *so* roast you if you try anything."

She grinned.

After a minute, so did he.

The bus rolled on through the dark, away from the castle, toward home.

URSULA VERNON (www.ursulavernon.com) is the award-winning creator of the Dragonbreath series. She lives, draws, and acts quite chivalrous in Pittsboro, North Carolina.